MOLEHOLE MYSTERIES

THE HARE-BRAINED HABIT

WRITTEN BY
Barbara Davoll
Pictures by Dennis Hockerman

MOODY PRESS
CHICAGO

Moody Press, a ministry of the Moody Bible Institute,
is designed for education, evangelization, and edifi-
cation. If we may assist you in knowing more about
Christ and the Christian life, please write us without
obligation: Moody Press, c/o MLM, Chicago, IL 60610.

ISBN: 0-8024-2705-7
PRINTED IN MEXICO

Children love the stories of Barbara Davoll, known for her award-winning, best-selling Christopher Churchmouse Classics and now for the Molehole Mystery series. Barbara writes these zany new adventures in Schroon Lake, New York, where she and her husband, Roy, minister at home and abroad with Word of Life International in their Missions Department. Barb manages to stay busy as a wife, mother, grandmother, author, drama teacher, church musician, and homemaker for her husband and Josh, the family Schnauzer.

Illustrator Dennis Hockerman has concentrated on art for children's trade books and textbooks, magazines, greeting cards, and games. He lives with his wife and three children in Mequon, Wisconsin, a suburb of Milwaukee. Mr. Hockerman probably spent more time "underground" than above while developing the characters and creating the etchings for the Molehole Mysteries. Periodically, he would poke his head into his "upstairs connection" to join his family and share with them the adventures of his friends in Molesbury R.F.D.

CARROT PATCH

DUSTY &
MUSTY MOLE HOME

MIGHTY MOLER
BALL
PARK

TROUBLED WATER BRIDGE

MOLESBURY
ELEMENTARY
SCHOOL

EAST FORK TUNNEL

MOLE HOLE
MYSTERY
CLUB

GYPSY CAMP

DIGGERTON →

N
W E
S

MUSTY

DUSTY

Contents

1. THE SLEEPYHEADS 9

2. WHAT'S WITH PENNEY? 17

3. PENNEY'S STRANGE BEHAVIOR 23

4. THE MONSTER 31

5. THE UPSTAIRS ARCADE 39

6. MUSTY'S BUS RIDE 47

7. THE BACK ROOM ADVENTURE 55

8. MUSTY'S STRANGE DISAPPEARANCE 63

9. MISS DUGGER'S ADVICE 71

10. THE UNDERGROUND ARCADE 79

THROUGH THE SPYGLASS 91

THE SLEEPYHEADS

Dusty Mole, junior agent of the Molehole Mystery Club, sat at his desk chewing a stub of pencil and thinking. He was hoping to finish his math assignment before the bell rang so he wouldn't have homework.

Across the aisle sat his twin sister and partner, Musty. She was also working hard. Just in front of Musty sat her mole friend, Penney.

"Did you get your problems finished?" Musty whispered to her.

There was no answer.

"Hey, Penney!" she whispered louder. "Did you get your problems finished?"

There was still no answer.

Leaning around her friend, Musty saw that Penney was sound asleep.

Giving Penney a poke in the back, Musty whispered loudly, "Hey, Penney, wake up! You'll never get this stuff done before Club tonight if you don't do most of it now."

Penney stirred and sat up, blinking her mole eyes. "What's up, Musty?" she asked, slurring her words in a funny sleepy daze.

Just then the teacher, Miss Dugger, turned around from writing an assignment on the chalkboard. "What did you say, Musty?"

Embarrassed to her toes, Musty didn't know what to say. She didn't want to repeat what she had said and get Penney into trouble. But Miss Dugger stood looking at her sternly.

"I-I said that we'd have to work hard to get this done before Club," replied Musty. Her conscience bothered her a bit that she didn't tell Miss Dugger she was trying to wake Penney.

"I thought I heard you say, 'Wake up,'" responded the teacher.

"Yes, ma'am, she did," agreed Penney. "I fell asleep. I'm sorry, Miss Dugger. I won't do it again," she said in an ashamed voice.

"Well, see that you don't, young lady. I can't teach you anything if you're asleep. You will have two extra problems to do for homework," she scolded. Miss Dugger turned and wrote the two additional problems on the board.

"Miss Dugger, Harey Rabbit's asleep too!" cried Seldon Shrew. He always liked to tattle and get the other animals in trouble if he could.

Miss Dugger turned from the board with an annoyed expression on her face. "HAREY!" she called loudly.

The little rabbit awoke with a jerk and jumped up from his seat. Thinking it was morning, he started to say the pledge to the flag. "I pledge allegiance..." he began.

The whole classroom erupted in laughter.

"HAREY! Sit down!" commanded Miss Dugger.

The class settled down with much snickering. Harey sank into his seat with an embarrassed look.

"You will all do these two extra problems also," reprimanded Miss Dugger.

Normally Miss Dugger was a very nice teacher, but today had not been a good day. Four of her students had fallen asleep in class. Miss Dugger seemed very relieved when the bell rang ending the day.

Harey, still sleepy, dropped his papers on the floor. Dusty, who already had his book bag packed, stepped across the aisle and helped the little rabbit pick them up.

"Here, Harey," he said kindly. "I'll help you."

Harey looked at Dusty and grabbed the papers. Stuffing them into his book bag he said roughly, "I don't need any help. I can manage by myself." Stumbling over Dusty's feet, he scrambled from the classroom.

Musty stood watching as the rabbit hurriedly left. "What's wrong with him?"

"Beats me," said her brother, scratching his head. "Sure isn't like him to act like that."

Musty turned to Penney, who was getting her books and homework stuff together. "I'll wait for you outside, Penney," she said. "I want to get a drink before we start home."

Penney was a member of the Molehole Mystery Club too, and the girl moles did everything together.

"Uh—you'd better go on ahead tonight," said Penney. "I've—uh—got stuff to do."

"Well, all right." Musty looked at her friend curiously. She and Penney always walked home together.

Something is wrong with Penney, Musty thought. *She just isn't acting like herself. I wonder what it can be?*

Since Penney wasn't with her, Musty walked home with her brother. Starting down the Underground tunnel that led toward their burrow, Dusty sighed. "Boy, I'm glad this day is over!"

"Me too," agreed Musty. "What is wrong with everyone? It's just September. They can't be tired of school yet."

"I know. I've been wondering what's up too. First Otis, then Morty, and now Harey and Penney all fall asleep in class."

"And did you notice they've all been grumpy too?"

"Yeah. Harey snapped at me when I tried to help him pick up his papers. He's usually a good kid."

"Wasn't that funny when he started to say the pledge?" Musty giggled.

"Funny is *right.*" Dusty chuckled. "But Miss Dugger didn't think so."

Musty sighed. "This is the first time Penney and I haven't walked home together. I don't understand all of this."

"Neither do I," responded the junior agent. "But I intend to find out. Something really strange is going on with them."

WHAT'S WITH PENNEY?

Later that evening Dusty called the Molehole Mystery Club members to order. "Before we begin I'll ask our secretary, Penney, to call the roll," he said in his junior agent voice.

There was a stir as the members looked around the clubhouse, expecting Penney to start calling their names. She was not there.

"Has anyone seen Penney this evening?" asked Dusty. "Perhaps she's just late." Sometimes the girl mole had chores to do for her mother.

"I haven't seen Penney much lately," responded Alby Mole.

"Neither have I," answered Millard Mole. "She's always with Musty. Surely she has seen her." He looked at Dusty's twin.

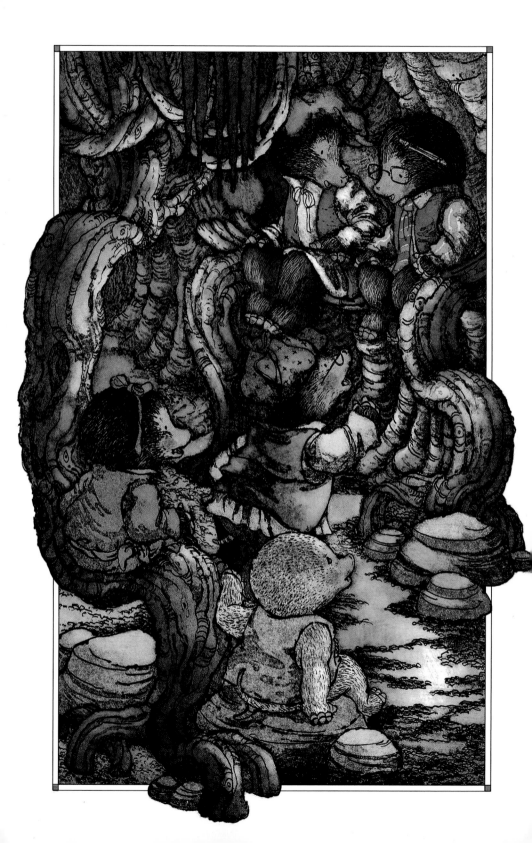

"I haven't seen Penney since school," responded Musty. "She wasn't waiting for me by the roots of the willow tree as usual. I guess she isn't coming."

"Well, she has the attendance book," stated Dusty. "Let's see who's missing." Taking a quick head count Dusty saw that two other members were missing. They were Otis and Mortimer.

"Has anyone seen Otis and Morty?" he asked.

"Nope," Snarkey answered. "Otis usually walks home from school with me, but he hasn't for the last week. I don't know where he is," he said with a frown.

"I haven't seen Mort either," added Millard. "He's usually the first one here. We always have time to throw a few balls while we wait for the rest of you."

"Something weird is going on," commented Dusty. "These three members of our club all fell asleep today in school."

The other club members nodded their heads.

"I wonder where they can be," he said.

"I don't know, but something else strange happened today," said Alby. "I asked Morty to help me do some work for Mr. Moriah. Usually he's glad to help him. But he said he wouldn't have time for that anymore. He was really jumpy and nervous too."

"I think we need to investigate this," said their leader. "Let's dispense with the rest of the meeting and see what we can find out. Just ask a few questions around Molesbury. Don't be too obvious," he warned. "Tomorrow night we'll meet again and see what we've discovered."

The club members left, going in different directions. Each of them had his clues notebook. Before tomorrow night they hoped they would know something more about the situation.

The next day at school started out to be a good one. All of Miss Dugger's students were alert in class, and she was in a much better mood.

There was no hint of trouble until early afternoon. The animals were busily working at their desks when suddenly Miss Dugger said, "Harey Rabbit, please come to my desk." She sounded so serious that the students looked up curiously.

Talking in a low voice, Miss Dugger was obviously scolding Harey. He hung his head sheepishly and scuffed his toes against the hard earth floor. When he returned to his seat he had several homework papers in his paw. The papers were covered with Miss Dugger's red marks. This was really surprising as Harey usually turned in perfect papers.

As the rabbit returned to his seat Miss Dugger said, "Penelope Mole, come to my desk, please."

Penney got up slowly and turned, looking at Musty with a curious look.

Musty shrugged her shoulders at Penney's unasked question. She didn't know what Miss Dugger wanted.

As the teacher began going over Penney's papers, the girl mole shifted from one foot to another. Miss Dugger's voice rose a little, and Musty could not help but overhear.

"Penelope, I am very surprised at you. This is a failing test in geography. You are one of the brightest students in the class. Didn't you study?"

Penney looked down at the floor and mumbled something, which Musty couldn't hear. Then Penney brushed her paw across her eyes.

"You may return to your seat," said Miss Dugger. "If this continues I will have to speak to your parents."

As Penney came back to her desk, her eyes avoided Musty's. She slumped into her seat. Musty could see her shoulders shaking and knew she was crying. She reached up to pat her friend's shoulder, but Penney shook her paw off. Penney didn't want to be comforted.

Musty felt as though she had been kicked in the stomach. She couldn't believe Penney would react that way to her. *What is wrong with my friend?* she thought sadly.

PENNEY'S
STRANGE BEHAVIOR

Before the day ended, Morty and Otis had also received serious scoldings from Miss Dugger. She gave a little talk to the whole class, saying that some students were not doing their best. She said it wasn't a good way to begin the school year. Parent-teacher conferences would be coming up soon, and she didn't want to have to give bad grades and comments on their report cards.

The whole class trooped out of the schoolroom feeling discouraged.

"I wish we all didn't get in trouble when some aren't doing well," complained Millard Mole to Dusty as they walked home.

"I know. It doesn't seem fair. But I'm sure she's trying to encourage us all to study and do our best," reflected Dusty. "Did you learn anything last evening when you did your questioning?"

"Not much," admitted Millard. "I checked on Harey Rabbit. The only rabbits at home in Haresville were the older ones. The younger rabbits were gone somewhere, and Harey's mother didn't know where they were."

"I don't like it," said Dusty. "There's more going on here than we think. Perhaps someone at Club will know more tonight."

But that night no one had any information about the situation.

"I don't like the idea of spying on our members," said Dusty. "But something has to be done. Penney is our secretary, and if she is dropping out of Club we need to know it."

Musty put up her hand to speak. "Dusty, may I be excused for a bit? I'll run by Penney's house and see where she is. Maybe I can bring her back and get her to talk to me."

"She'd better be home studying, from what Miss Dugger said today," observed Snarkey.

Musty shot a warning look at him. *Snarkey had better watch his step,* she thought loyally. *Even if it's true, he doesn't need to talk about it.*

Dusty gave his approval for Musty to leave, and she scampered from the clubhouse. As she wound her way along the overgrown path that led to the Molesbury tunnel, her heart lightened a bit. Penney would probably be at home studying. She'd be able to talk to her and straighten out all this mess.

When Musty knocked on the little burrow door where her friend lived, Penney's mother answered the door.

"Why, hello, Musty," she said pleasantly. "I haven't seen you all week. I thought you were having an extra session of the Mystery Club tonight."

"We are," replied Musty. "I just came over to see where Penney is. I thought maybe she didn't know about it."

"Isn't Penney at Club?" asked her mother in a surprised voice.

"No, she isn't. She didn't come last evening either."

"Why, that's really strange," said Penney's mother. "She came home after school and tore upstairs to get something. She said you had an emergency meeting and she wouldn't be home for supper. Are you sure she isn't in Club?"

"No, ma'am. Penney hasn't been to our meetings last night or tonight."

"Where can she be?" Penney's mother asked in a distracted tone.

"I wish I knew," Musty said sadly. "Do you know where her attendance notebook is for Club? I guess I'll have to be the secretary till she comes back."

"I think it's right upstairs in her room," said the worried mole mother. "Come on up with me, and I'll get it for you."

Musty followed Penney's mom up the steps to her friend's familiar room. She and Penney always had such fun playing up here.

Mrs. Mole gasped as she opened Penney's door. The room was a mess! Clothes were strewn everywhere, drawers were pulled out, and everything was upside down. Lying in the corner were her forgotten schoolbooks.

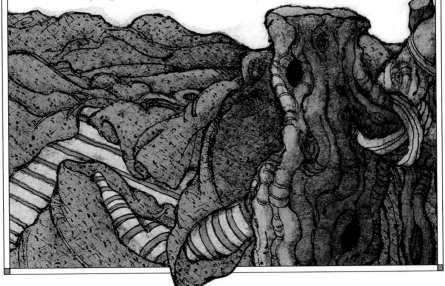

"Why, I can't imagine what has come over Penney!" exclaimed her mother.

"Neither can I," muttered Musty as she took the notebook Penney's mom found under a heap of clothes on the bed.

THE MONSTER

Later, as the twin moles walked home from Club, Musty told her brother what she had learned at Penney's house. She knew Dusty would keep it quiet and use the information to find out what was going on with their friends.

"I'm really worried," she said. "It's not like Penney to leave her room in such a mess."

"You know, sis, I think I'll follow Otis tomorrow after school and see where he goes," said Dusty thoughtfully. "Maybe they are all doing something together, and we can find out what it is."

"I don't know if that's a good idea," argued Musty. "I sure hate to spy on my friends."

"I don't like it either, Musty. But whatever they're up to can't be good. They've all changed so much—and not for the better. I think it's the only way to help them."

"Well, if you think so," she agreed. "I guess it is important enough to do that. Penney lied to her mother about going to Club, and that is very serious."

The next evening after school, Dusty waited in the classroom until Otis was safely outside. Then he followed the chubby mole down the tunnel that led to his home.

Otis stopped at the store and bought some candy grubs for a snack. Dusty smiled as he saw his friend stuff his mouth full of them. Otis sure liked to eat.

When Otis finished his treat, he started off again. Instead of heading toward his own home, he turned at the fork of the tunnel that led to Haresville.

That's strange, thought Dusty as he followed him. *Haresville is where all the rabbits live.* Then he remembered that Harey Rabbit was one of the students that had fallen asleep in class. *I wonder if he's going to Harey's house?*

Just then Dusty heard voices behind him in the tunnel. Turning off the path to Haresville, he hid behind some roots and waited. He watched quietly, and the voices came closer. *It's Penney and Morty! Maybe they are going to Harey's too,* he thought.

Penney and Morty were walking quickly and soon were almost out of sight. Dusty slipped back onto the tunnel path and followed them.

As the animals approached the village of Haresville, Otis was waiting for them. The three walked on together to Harey's house. Harey joined them, and they headed for the Upstairs Connection.

The Connection was a long tunnel leading straight up through the ground to the Upstairs, aboveground.

I wonder where they are going, worried Dusty.

When he stepped through the hole to the Upstairs, he squinted in the late afternoon sun. It was always risky for moles to be aboveground, as they didn't see very well. Whatever his friends were doing up here was dangerous. The Upstairs was not a safe place for underground animals.

At first Dusty thought he had lost sight of his four friends. But when his eyes grew accustomed to the light, he saw them walking rapidly down the road ahead.

They must be crazy, he thought, *to walk right down the road openly like that. Don't they know how dangerous it is up here?*

Just then a dark shadow from overhead came across the road. Dusty quickly darted into the bushes nearby. Looking up, he saw the shadow was that of a huge black hawk, who was circling slowly.

That hawk is looking for his supper, he thought. *I sure hope he doesn't catch me or one of my friends.* Hawks were the worst enemy he knew. Without any warning they could swoop down, catch an unsuspecting small animal in their huge claws, and fly away to feast on it.

The hawk continued circling above the heads of his friends. Dusty shuddered as he watched. They didn't even seem to notice the big bird. They were talking and intent on where they were going. To Dusty's relief, the hawk flew away.

After walking for some time, Dusty saw big buildings in the distance and knew they were approaching the city. The detective mole had never been near the big city before. His parents had always warned him and Musty about the terrible dangers there.

As they walked on, the dusty country path became a black strip of road. *This must be the highway Father Malcolm told me about,* he thought. His father had warned him about the highway and how dangerous it was. Dusty saw that Penney, Morty, Otis, and Harey were walking right down the middle of the road.

Suddenly the mole heard a terrific roar. He looked behind him, and his fur stood straight up. A big monster was racing down the road toward him.

Dusty quickly jumped off into the ditch that ran along the highway. It was none too soon, for the huge monster came roaring by, throwing rocks and gravel as it passed.

With his heart pounding wildly, he scrambled up the bank to see the monster bearing down on his friends. They were still in the middle of the road, not knowing that death was stalking them.

Dusty watched in horror as the monster flew toward his friends. His tongue clung dryly to the roof of his mouth as he realized there was no way to warn them of the danger. They could not hear him. The little mole buried his face in his hands, not daring to look.

THE UPSTAIRS ARCADE

As Harey Rabbit walked along with the three moles, they talked excitedly. Morty threw back his head and laughed at a joke Harey was telling. Suddenly Morty heard a deafening roar. Looking over his shoulder he saw the monster speeding toward them.

With a scream he grabbed Penney and Otis, pulling them to safety at the edge of the road. Harey hopped to the side. The little moles clung fearfully to each other as the awful thing sped by. The rabbit stood laughing at them.

"Oh, what was that?" cried Penney, shaking all over with fear.

"Aw, don't be such babies," scoffed Harey. "That's just a truck! If you guys are going to be such fraidies, I'm not taking you a step farther."

"We're not afraid," insisted Morty. "We've just never seen a truck that close before. Let's go." With that the four animals resumed walking toward the city.

Meanwhile, behind them, Dusty couldn't believe his eyes. They were safe! He felt weak all over from fear of what could have happened.

What is wrong with them? he thought with disgust. *They were nearly killed, and it hasn't bothered them one bit. Where can they be going that is important enough to take such risks?* The detective mole continued to follow curiously.

They walked for what seemed a terribly long time. Dusty noticed that they were in the heart of the city now. He felt much safer up on the sidewalk than on the highway.

Suddenly the animals ahead came to a stop in front of a building that had a large, flashing, red sign. Dusty could read the letters as they flashed. "ARCADE." Although he could read the word he didn't know what an arcade was. Harey started into an alley beside the building, and the moles followed. They acted as though they knew where they were going.

The animals went to a side door and darted through when someone came out. Dusty was right behind them. The junior agent found himself in a dimly lit, noisy room.

In a few seconds his eyes adjusted, and he saw lots of young people standing in front of some machines with bright lights. The machines made strange noises.

As he watched from behind a trash can, he saw that the kids were putting money into the machines. *I think they're playing a game,* he thought. That seemed funny to Dusty. He loved to play games, but he always played them with his friends or his sister.

These kids all seem to be playing alone, he thought. *I don't think that would be much fun.* Each of the kids stayed in front of the game machine a long time. When one left, another stepped up to play. *They don't even talk with each other,* thought Dusty. *People sure do strange things.*

Enough of this, he thought. *I've got to find my friends.* The private eye scurried among the legs of the people, who paid no attention at all to him. They were totally into their games.

Finally Dusty spotted them. The three moles were perched on top of a high counter looking down on a game machine near them. Harey sat on top of a high trash can nearby.

In the darkness the junior agent found it easy to scramble up and hide himself in a large display card on the counter.. Here, he was able to sit very close to his friends and hear their conversation without their seeing him.

"Now watch this," called Harey to the moles. "This kid will do better than the last one. I've seen him play lots of times. He's really good."

Dusty leaned out so that he could see better. The boy put his money into the machine and started to play.

Although Dusty didn't know exactly how to play the game, it didn't take him long to figure out that the boy was very good. The points he racked up on the screen climbed into the thousands. The boy kept pouring money into the machine.

These kids must be rich, thought Dusty. The boy's friends cheered each time he did well. The noise in the Arcade was deafening.

Dusty looked at his mole friends, who seemed to be having the time of their lives watching everything. He saw Harey open a knapsack he had brought and pass out some tiny sandwiches to the animals. Dusty was hungry. He wished he could have one. But he must not let them know he was there.

He heard Morty say, "I brought some money, Harey. Why can't we play?"

"Nah, it's too dangerous. If they catch us we won't be able to come up and watch anymore. We should go now," he added and jumped down. "But remember, I told you I'm working on getting some games for us. In two days we'll have our own arcade underground. Let's go."

Dusty waited until the animals had left the arcade. Then he scooted out the door when it opened and began to follow them the long way back to the Underground.

How is Harey going to open an arcade underground? he wondered. *Where will he get the game machines?* Somehow the little mole thought he didn't want to know.

MUSTY'S BUS RIDE

Although Dusty had told his parents he would be late, Mother Miranda was not expecting him to be as late as he was. When he opened the door to their burrow, she was still up waiting for him. She laid aside her knitting and came over to greet him.

"Oh, son, I've been worried. You've never been late like this before."

"I know, Mother. I'm sorry. I knew you would be worried. I followed Morty, Penney, and Otis to find out why they've been acting so strange lately. It was quite a trip Upstairs." He sighed.

"Upstairs! It's so dangerous up there, Dusty. Did you find out anything?"

"Well, Harey Rabbit took them. I guess they go up there every evening."

"Every evening!" gasped his mother. "What on earth for?"

"They go to the Arcade. It's a place where the young kids Upstairs play games. There is a big building full

of game machines. The kids up there play for hours at a time. It was fun to watch."

"But Dusty—every evening? How are the moles getting their homework done?"

"That's just it. They aren't," responded her son. He told his mother how his friends had been falling asleep in class and failing in their grades.

Dusty's mother sat down in her chair and listened carefully as Dusty talked. When he finished she shook her head sadly.

"It's hard to believe Penney's mother would allow her to do such a dangerous thing," she said.

"I don't think she knows," added Dusty. Then he told her what Musty had discovered when she went to Penney's house.

"That is very serious, Dusty," Mother Miranda said. "That means Penney lied to her mother. I wonder what her mother thinks about her being so late tonight."

"I don't know, but I know I'm very tired. And I still have to study for a test tomorrow."

"Oh no, dear. You need to go to bed. I'll wake you a bit early in the morning to study. You get right to sleep now," insisted his mother.

The next morning Dusty walked to school slowly. He was still very tired and did not feel well prepared for his test. With a sigh he placed his earthworm sandwich on the shelf in the coat room and took his place at his desk. He wished he could put his head down and sleep, but he resisted the urge. *No wonder my friends fell asleep in school,* he thought.

When Miss Dugger began class, Morty and Otis were still absent. Penney had come in just as the bell rang, and Harey came in as they were saying the pledge to the flag.

In the middle of math class Morty came into the schoolroom and handed Miss Dugger his tardy excuse. When he slipped into his seat, Dusty smiled at him. Morty nodded and smiled tiredly.

Dusty thought the day would never end. As soon as the dismissal bell rang he hurriedly put his books away so that he could get home as soon as possible. He could hardly wait to take a nap.

As he was leaving the classroom he heard Miss Dugger talking to Harey. "Did you study for this test at all?" she asked. Dusty couldn't hear Harey's answer, but he was pretty sure the rabbit hadn't studied.

Musty was waiting outside for Dusty. "Is Otis sick, Dusty?" she asked.

"I don't know," Dusty sighed. Then he told Musty all that had happened the night before.

"Why don't we go see if Otis is all right?" suggested Musty anxiously.

"I can't, Musty. I'm so tired I have to take a nap. You can go if you want. Or I'll go with you when I wake up," her brother said.

Musty decided to go while Dusty was napping. When she got there, his mother said that Otis was not feeling well and was resting. Musty asked her to tell him she had called and hoped he would feel better soon. As the little girl mole left his home she felt very discouraged.

Nothing is fun anymore, she thought. *Everyone is always busy or sleeping. Maybe I should call on Penney and see if she can come over and play.* When she rang the bell at Penney's house her friend's mother answered the door.

"I'm sorry, Musty. Penney is sleeping. She was so tired after school she went right to bed."

Leaving Penney's house, Musty decided she would go to Harey's. Maybe she could talk some sense into him. He just couldn't keep on dragging their friends around at night. With determination she walked toward Haresville. She had to do something to help the situation.

As Musty came in sight of Harey's house she saw him come out of his house and start down the road toward the Upstairs Connection. He had his book bag on his back.

She decided she would follow him and see what he was up to. *Dusty will be glad for anything I can find out*, she thought.

Harey hurried down the road, not knowing he was being followed. When he got to the Upstairs Connection he entered without hesitation. He was heading for the Upstairs again. Although Musty had not received permission to leave the Underground, she followed the rabbit.

When Harey left the Underground this time, he didn't walk on the highway. He walked down the road for a few feet and stopped under a sign that said "BUS STOP."

Musty hung back and watched. Several people came and stood there also. Soon she saw the bus coming. Musty had seen one of those before, when she and Mother Miranda had been Upstairs. She knew all of the people would get on it and ride.

Musty stayed toward the back of the crowd getting on the bus. She saw Harey scramble aboard. Just before the door closed she jumped aboard also and stayed on the floor close to the door. She didn't want Harey to see her. The little mole's heart was pounding wildly. She was doing a scary thing, and she knew her parents would not approve.

I just have to find out more about this, she thought. *Somehow I have to help Penney and the others.* Musty could not imagine what lay ahead or where her bus ride would take her.

THE BACK ROOM ADVENTURE

As Musty rode along on the bus she realized that she couldn't see the back door. Harey could get off back there, and she wouldn't know it. The mole decided she had to get up into the aisle so she could see better. Jumping up from the step by the door, she landed close to the driver. Quickly she darted under some people's feet and headed toward the back of the bus.

Sure enough, she spotted the rabbit sitting on the floor behind a person wearing some big white sneakers. *Harey's pretty smart,* she thought. His white fur blended right in with the boy's shoes. She had always known Harey was smart, because he made such good grades in school. *I'm not sure it's smart for him to be playing around up here though,* she thought.

They rode for such a long time that Musty found herself getting sleepy. Suddenly someone rang the bell, which meant people wanted to get off.

Musty was alert instantly, watching Harey. She saw him move a bit, getting ready to jump when the door opened. Quickly the girl mole darted in and out of the feet and poised ready to jump off too.

Harey jumped right in front of an older lady who took a long time getting off.

Now's my chance, Musty thought as Harey jumped off. Just as the lady stepped down on the bottom step, Musty jumped.

The woman gasped and nearly lost her balance when she saw the mole and the rabbit.

I sure hope she's all right, worried Musty. She liked people a lot and thought they were very interesting. Landing on the sidewalk, Musty looked frantically around for Harey. Busy people hurried up and down the street.

Musty kept trying to dodge feet while looking for
the rabbit. Suddenly she saw him. He was hopping
down the sidewalk, avoiding the people's big feet. It
looked dangerous to Musty, but she thought if he could
do it, she could too.

In no time the mole had the hang of it. The trick was
to zigzag among the people walking and not stay in
one place more than a second or two. Keeping track
of Harey wasn't hard. The white rabbit was easy to spot
among the people's feet.

I wonder how far he's going? thought the mole. She
was out of breath trying to keep up with him. Just then
she spotted a big sign ahead. It blinked: "ARCADE."

There it is, she thought with excitement. *Just like Dusty said.* But to her disappointment, Harey didn't turn in at the Arcade. Instead he went on by that building to one several doors down the street. He stopped and looked up at the storefront. A sign in the window said: "Electronic Hand Games Sold Here."

Musty stopped close to the building and waited for Harey to make his next move. Instead of going in the front door of the store, the rabbit went around to the back and hopped up on a trash can that was sitting under an open window. From the trash can Harey jumped to the window sill and slid through into the back of the store.

Musty gasped. *What is he doing now?* Not wanting to lose sight of him, she followed and slithered through the window as well. She could tell they were in the back of the store. There were stacks and stacks of boxes. No one seemed to be around.

Musty hid behind some boxes, looking for Harey. Soon she saw him. He was on top of an open box and had one of the electronic games in his paw. He was stuffing it into his book bag.

So that's what he's up to, thought the mole in shock. *He's stealing those games from the store.* She was ready to yell at Harey and tell him to stop when she heard someone coming. Before she could do anything, a huge motor started up, and someone shouted.

"Move that stack of boxes!" the voice yelled.

The loud sound of the motor came closer and closer. Musty saw a whole stack of boxes being moved. They were going to pile the boxes on top of her!

The girl mole didn't know which way to jump. "Harey!" she screamed. But he couldn't hear her above the sound of the motor. Musty knew she had to do something, or she would be buried alive. Closing her eyes she jumped, hoping she could get out of the way of the boxes that were coming down on her.

As she jumped, Musty fell and struck something hard. A sharp pain in her head paralyzed her and everything went black. Dropping to the floor the little mole lay where she fell.

Several hours passed and darkness came. When Musty came to, there was no sound of a motor. In fact, there were no sounds at all. She sat up and looked around in a dazed way. *Where am I?* she wondered. Putting her paw up to her head she touched a big bump.

"Oooh," she groaned. Now she remembered. She had followed Harey, and boxes were being stacked on top of her. But where was Harey?

Slowly, as her brain cleared, Musty realized that the store was closed. And Harey was gone. The little girl mole was near panic. She had no idea how to find her way back to the Underground without Harey. *What will I do now?* she wondered frantically.

The little mole scrambled around in the back room looking for the window where they had entered. When she found it she discovered it was tightly locked. Fear came over Musty in a great wave. She was trapped.

MUSTY'S DISAPPEARANCE

When Dusty awoke from his nap, Mother Miranda asked him if he knew where his sister was. She hadn't come home from school yet.

"She was going to drop by and see if Otis is all right. He didn't come to school today," explained her brother. "I'm sure she'll be home soon."

Dusty began his homework. He had several things to do, since he had neglected his studies the night before. Soon he could smell Mother Miranda's good cooking and knew supper was almost ready. Walking into the kitchen he grabbed a pawful of turnip greens from the salad Mother was preparing and stuffed them into his mouth.

"Musty still isn't home," said Mother. "Why don't you run over and get her? Your father will be home in a few minutes, and supper will be ready."

When he got there, Dusty was surprised to find that Otis was in bed.

"Musty was here right after school, but she didn't stay when I told her Otis wasn't feeling well," explained the chubby mole's mother.

Before going home, Dusty stopped at Penney's and was told the same thing. He checked at several other homes where he knew his sister often visited. No one had seen her.

Dusty returned home, and he and his family ate dinner hoping that Musty would return any minute. When she didn't come, Dusty's parents became very concerned.

"This just isn't like Musty," worried Mother Miranda. "She is always so good to ask me if she can go somewhere."

Dusty didn't say it, but he was worried also. He knew Musty would never miss supper without permission. "Don't worry, Mom. I'll look for her. I'll be back in no time. She probably just lost track of the time."

Father Malcolm said that he would look for her too. As father and son left their burrow, Father Malcolm told Dusty he would search the Underground toward the town of Diggerton. "You go the other way, Dusty, toward Haresville."

Dusty asked at every burrow along the road toward Haresville. No one had seen his sister. When he came to Harey's house, he knocked politely. After a bit Harey came to the door.

"Uh, hello, Dusty. What can I do for you?" asked the rabbit.

"I'm looking for my sister, Harey. Have you seen her?" By now Dusty was really worried and didn't take any time for small talk.

"Why, no, I haven't," said Harey. "Is she missing?"

"She hasn't come home from school yet, and that isn't like her," admitted Dusty. "You're sure you haven't seen her?" He looked at Harey intently. Somehow he just didn't trust the rabbit since Harey had taken his other friends Upstairs into such danger.

"No, I sure haven't. I'll be glad to help you look for her though," he said helpfully.

"No, thanks," responded Dusty. "I'm sure she'll be home when I get there. Thanks, anyway." Dusty didn't want to arouse any more curiosity about Musty than necessary.

He returned home to find that his father had learned nothing about Musty.

Mother Miranda sat on the couch dabbing her eyes with her hanky. "Oh, Malcolm, where can my little girl be?" she cried.

"There, there, my dear," comforted Father. "She's probably doing something for the Mystery Club."

"But Dusty would know if that's the case," she reasoned. "You don't suppose she could have gone Upstairs?" asked Mother Miranda frantically. "It's so dangerous up there for a mole, and it's very late at night."

"Now you know Musty wouldn't do that without permission," Father assured her.

Dusty stood looking at his parents. "She wouldn't if she thought about it," he said. "But perhaps..." His voice trailed off as he thought about his sister and what she would do if she thought she had a clue.

Father looked at Dusty. "What do you mean, son?" he asked urgently.

Dusty hesitated. He didn't want to worry his parents needlessly. But there was a chance that Musty could have found a clue that would lead her Upstairs. Then she might forget to ask permission.

"Do you think Musty could be Upstairs?" questioned the worried father.

Quickly Dusty explained what he thought and then convinced his parents that he and Snarkey Mole should check out the Upstairs. Surely they would find Musty at the Arcade looking for clues.

But the hard trip Upstairs revealed nothing to the moles. Musty was not at the Arcade. They returned to the Underground very discouraged. The long night of Musty's disappearance turned to morning, and the little girl mole was still missing.

Father insisted Dusty go to school, but he couldn't concentrate on his studies. Miss Dugger kindly told him he could go home early in the morning. As he was getting his things together, Penney asked Miss Dugger if she could speak to Dusty.

Following him into the coat room, Penney began to cry. "This is all my fault, Dusty," she said, crying as though her heart would break. "I've paid no attention to Musty at all lately. Harey has been taking us Upstairs—"

"I know that, Penney. And Musty has missed your friendship," he interrupted.

"She's probably run away," Penney burst out. "And it's all my fault!"

MISS DUGGER'S ADVICE

Penney was crying so hard that Miss Dugger heard her and came into the coatroom to see what was the matter. Dusty stood patting Penney on the shoulder awkwardly.

"She thinks it's her fault that Musty is missing," he explained.

Just then Morty poked his head around the corner of the coatroom. "It's not just her fault. It's mine too," he said sadly.

Then Otis walked into the crowded coatroom. Wiping his paw across his eyes he added, "You're not alone. She came to see me last night when she thought I was sick. I didn't even get up, because I was too tired from the night before. If something has happened to Musty I'm to blame too."

Miss Dugger looked at the sad students standing in front of her. Something had to be done. She couldn't continue school like this.

"Wait just a minute, students, and we'll talk about all of this," she said.

Miss Dugger walked out of the coatroom and dismissed the rest of the students. She told them she was giving them the day off to help find Musty. Then she called the others to come and sit down in the classroom to have a talk.

The time with Miss Dugger was really helpful. Morty, Otis, and Penney were honest with their teacher. They explained what had been going on with Harey.

"Speaking of Harey, where is he?" questioned Miss Dugger. "He's absent today."

"I don't know," said Dusty. "He was all right last night when I saw him at home. I stopped to see if Musty was there."

"Hmm," Miss Dugger said. "Maybe you and your Mystery Club should check on him today. Perhaps he knew more than he told you. But before you go—let me give you all one piece of advice," she added. "I'm sure you know there is nothing at all wrong with playing games. But life cannot be all play. When we do one thing too often and it interferes with everything else in life, then it becomes wrong. It is not wrong in itself, but only wrong when it keeps us from doing what we know is good and right.

"I think you all know that excessive game playing is wrong. It has kept you from your studies, your friendships, and even from your Mystery Club work, which has been such a help to the Underground. Now in some way it may have even led to Musty's disappearance.

"I've given you the day off to hopefully find Musty. I also hope you will find your way back to being my responsible, caring students again.

"I want you to know I love each one of you and am here to help in any way that I can." These last words were said brokenly as Miss Dugger wiped her eyes. "I too will be looking for our dear little Musty," she said.

Penney went to Miss Dugger and gave her a hug. "Please forgive me, Miss Dugger," she said with a sob. "I've been acting like a brat." Miss Dugger smiled and said she forgave her.

Morty and Otis solemnly shook her paw and asked for forgiveness also. Dusty stood by awkwardly, waiting for them to join in the search for Musty.

The reunited friends headed first for the Molehole Mystery Club shack. Alby, Millard, Snarkey, and Alfred Mole, the other members, were already there waiting for them.

"We figured there would be an emergency meeting," explained Alby. "We came just as soon as Miss Dugger dismissed school."

Dusty's heart was heavy with concern for his sister, but he made a brave little speech about how good it was to have the Club back together.

"Now I'll ask our secretary, Penney Mole, to read any clues that she has for our new business—the—uh— disappearance of Musty Mole."

It was a good thing Dusty didn't have to say anything more, for the lump in his throat was making speech very difficult.

It seemed that none of the members had any further clues about Musty to report.

Suddenly, Morty jumped to his feet. "I don't have any clues about Musty, but I just remembered something Harey said," he exclaimed. "He said that in two days we would have our own Underground arcade. I don't know what he meant, but maybe we should check it out."

"Thank you, Mort," said Dusty. "Write that down, Penney. If there is nothing further, I think we should split up in teams. Alby and Millard, you go together. Otis and Snarkey, you two pair up, and Morty, you and I—and Penney," he directed. "We'll meet back here at four o'clock this afternoon with any clues we can find."

The animals formed a ring and extended their paws in the old Mystery Club handshake. "CLUEHOUSE," they said in unison. It felt good to be reunited once again. But none of the animals felt good about this mystery. It wasn't fun to be looking for one of their own.

THE UNDERGROUND ARCADE

Dusty, Morty, and Penney decided they would go immediately to Harey's. They wanted to check out Morty's clue. When they reached Harey's house he was up on a ladder hanging a sign that said "UNDERGROUND ARCADE."

"Hey, Harey," called the junior agent to the rabbit. The rabbit turned around, still holding the sign. He had a nail clenched in his teeth.

"We'd like to talk to you about my sister."

Harey nodded and mumbled something they couldn't understand. He took the nail out of his mouth and pounded it into the sign. Then he hopped down from the ladder and joined them.

"I heard you haven't found her yet, Dusty," said Harey. "I'm sorry about that."

"There are some things you need to know, Harey," said Morty, taking the lead. "Dusty followed us the last time we went to the Arcade."

"Why did you do that?" asked the rabbit. "You could have gone with us if you'd asked."

"Uh—he didn't want to go with us, Harey. He followed us to see why we were all acting so funny. You see, Otis and Penney and I are all members of the Molehole Mystery Club. None of us were showing up for Club and—"

"And all of you were falling asleep in school and acting weird," interrupted Dusty. "I couldn't imagine what was changing you from good students to failing and why you were so grumpy. Penney wasn't friendly to Musty anymore, and lots of things made me want to know what was up," explained the junior agent.

"Yeah, well, now you know we've found something better than the old Molehole Mystery Club." Harey waved a paw at the new sign. "We're going to have an arcade down here. 'Course we won't have the big machines, but it won't cost as much either."

"We'll have the small hand-held games, and the animals will only have to pay five cents a game. You can come and play too," he added generously to Dusty.

"Well, right now we have to look for my friend Musty," said Penney, who had been standing quietly listening. "I don't think I'll be playing too much, Harey. I've really been slipping a lot in my studies. Now that Musty's missing, I've realized how much she meant to me. I think it's more fun to play together than with a machine."

"Don't get us wrong, Harey. We appreciate your showing us the Arcade and all," said Morty. "We've just decided that we can't let it take up all our time."

"Wait a minute, you two," said the rabbit with a sneer. "I went to a lot of trouble to get these games for you, and now you aren't going to use them? How am I going to make any money?"

"Morty said they would play some, Harey," said Dusty. "And I'm sure others will too, once they know you have the games. You'll make enough to cover the cost you had in buying them."

Suddenly Harey became very quiet. Looking down at his feet, he said, "Oh sure, I'll make enough to pay for them, I guess." Clearing his throat he added, "Well, I sure hope you find Musty. I have some work to do to get set up by tonight. By the way, how did you get away from that ogre Miss Dugger?"

"Miss Dugger is not an ogre," said Penney in an indignant tone. "She gave us the day off to look for Musty. Some of us don't *skip* school," she said flatly.

"Uh—yes—well, we'll be going now," said Dusty, putting a firm paw on Penney's shoulder. He didn't want them to get into a serious fuss with Harey.

"No, we won't be going yet," said a familiar voice from behind them. None of the animals had seen the missing Musty approaching from around the new arcade.

"Musty!" screeched Penney, whirling around and grabbing her friend in a joyous hug. "Oh, Musty, where were you? We've all been so worried."

"Yeah, where *were* you, sis? Mom and Dad are worried sick over you." Now that his sister was here, Dusty found himself not only relieved, but a little angry that she could worry them so.

"I know they've been worried. I've just seen them, and I've apologized to them for all the trouble I've caused. I've been Upstairs locked in the back of a store that sells electronic hand games." She looked fiercely at Harey.

Harey was a white rabbit, but suddenly he seemed pale, and his nose began to quiver nervously.

"Wh-where?" he stammered.

"You ought to know, Harey. I saw you there when you *stole* the electronic games which I suppose you're using to set up your arcade here." Musty nodded toward the new sign.

"*STOLE!*" said Morty and Dusty in unison. They stared at their rabbit friend in unbelief.

Harey dropped his head in shame. "Yeah, I guess I did," he mumbled. "I thought they wouldn't miss them, and I could make some money to buy a really big machine."

Dusty shook his head sadly as he looked at Harey. *Did the poor foolish rabbit actually think he could get a machine of that size underground?*

Out loud he said, "Your reasoning isn't logical, Harey. I thought you were a *smart* rabbit. You surely knew you couldn't do that. A big machine like that would never fit down the Upstairs Connection."

"Oh, I know that," responded Harey. "But I'd figured out how to make the machines work. I could have gotten the parts and brought them down a piece at a time."

"And stolen that stuff too?" sneered Morty. "For a smart animal you sure aren't using your head!"

"This is just what Miss Dugger was talking about," said Penney. "She said there's nothing wrong with playing games as long as it doesn't interfere with your life and the things you know are right. You've just gotten off on the wrong track, Harey."

"Look, I've an idea," suggested Dusty. "Why don't we all help Harey take these games back where they belong? I think we have enough dues in the Mystery Club bank to buy one game. If we buy one we could keep it here and have some rules about using it. How does all that sound to you, Harey?" questioned Dusty.

The rabbit had stood quietly listening to them. No one knew what he was thinking. "Do you mean you aren't going to tell anyone I stole these games?" he asked in surprise.

"No, *we* aren't going to tell anyone," said Dusty quietly. "But *you* need to take the games back to the store and tell the manager what you've done. We'll go with you," he added.

Harey looked at the Molehole Mystery gang. Suddenly he was very ashamed. Swallowing hard he said, "I—I guess you guys are right. You know, I used to think your Club was all a big joke. Now I see you're a pretty good bunch. If I were a mole I think I'd like to join you."

"We might make an exception for a rabbit like you, Harey." Dusty laughed. "I mean after all, you're *smart* enough to join."

The others laughed.

Then Harey turned toward his arcade. "Let's get these games returned before it gets dark."

"I'll be right back," called Musty. "I have to go ask permission to go Upstairs."

The animals laughed again as Musty started toward her home.

"I'll go with her to make sure she doesn't come up missing again," said Penney, giggling.

None of the moles were looking forward to facing the store manager, but they knew it was the right thing to do.

Later, as they returned to the Underground, they felt much lighter and grateful the manager had been understanding about Harey's stealing.

"I guess we all learned some valuable lessons today," observed Musty.

Otis, who had been looking in his pockets for something to eat, pulled out a sticky candy grub and stuffed it into his mouth. "*UMMHMM*," chortled the chubby mole, with his mouth full. "I learned to always buy extra grubs. You never know when you might need them."

The Molehole gang all laughed. Things were getting back to normal, and that seemed great. They were excited to see what next adventure awaited them in the game of life.

THROUGH THE SPYGLASS

The moles had a scary adventure when they fell into the trap of excessive game playing. Let's see how they have handled the problem now that some time has elapsed.

We see all of the Molehole Mystery Club gang happily going about their studies at school. Miss Dugger was very helpful in allowing them to make up their failing work and tests. Soon they were settled into their normal routine, and the falling asleep in class stopped.

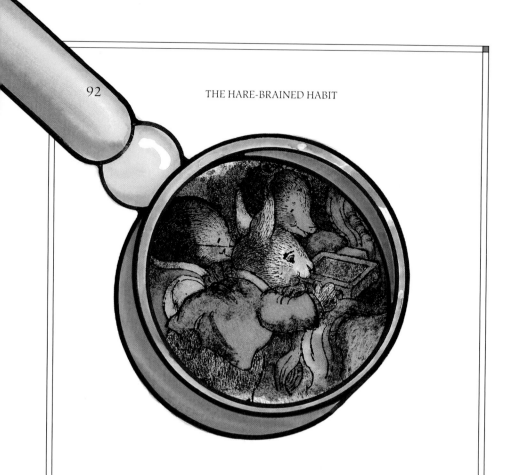

Harey, along with the others, returned the games to the store and made things right with the manager. The Molehole Mystery Club bought one game with their dues, and some rules were posted above it. These are the rules they decided would help them:

1. All homework must be done before playing games.
2. No one may play more than three games in a row.
3. Scores are to be recorded so that healthy competition is encouraged.
4. There will be no charge for playing the games.

Sometimes it is easy to let something take over our lives. We can get so wrapped up in it that we forget everything else, including our studies, family, and friends. This is true of electronic games, television, sports, and even reading.

There is so much to do today that is good. There are some excellent programs on television, and our computer age is fascinating. However, we must be certain that the things that interest us are things that please God and will uplift and strengthen us.

Colossians 3:17 says, "Whatever you do, whether in word or deed, do it all in the name of the Lord Jesus, giving thanks to God the Father through him" *(New International Version)*.

We should be very careful to avoid television and reading material that is harmful and degrading. Another excellent verse for us to remember is found in Psalm 101:2. It says, "I will be careful to lead a blameless life" *(New International Version)*. If we do this, we can be sure our lives will be pleasing to God.

UNDERGROUND
"DIG-TIONARY"

RABBIT (rab'it): A small long-eared mammal of the hare family (*Webster's New Collegiate Dictionary*).

Don't you just love little rabbits with their cute round faces and long ears? They are one of the Lord's creations that live underground in burrows. Almost half of their time is spent underground.

A father rabbit is called a buck. A mother rabbit is called a doe. That is just the same as the deer family. But—listen to this—the baby rabbits are called kittens. Isn't that funny? It's easy to see why, though. They are soft and furry just like baby kittens.

Papa Rabbit doesn't do much of the housework. In fact, he doesn't even do much of the digging of the burrow. His job is to be a father and to protect his home and family.

Usually two to six "kittens" are born at a time in a

nest that the mother rabbit has made. Mama Rabbit takes good care of her babies until they are a month or two old. By then they are able to go aboveground and graze for their food.

Often young rabbits can be seen sitting in the doorway of their burrow taking a sunbath while their parents are grazing nearby. When they graze, or eat, rabbits "chew the cud" just like a cow. This means they chew their digested food again and again.

Rabbits are good little youngsters because they like their vegetables. You would never hear them say "Yuck" to a nice bunch of broccoli or lettuce. That is what they love. In fact, they must have green food to live.

Rabbits don't live very long—usually only 18 to 20 months. But they have a very active life in their short time on earth. Can you imagine how many rabbits there would be in the world if they didn't die at a young age? Since each mother may have up to 30 babies a year, the world would soon be overrun with rabbits.

Hares, although of the same family, are usually larger than rabbits. There are 30 species of hares and 26 different species of rabbits. A close study of these interesting little animals shows again how the Lord wonderfully cares for His creation.

JOIN
MOLEHOLE MYSTERY CLUB

Would you like to join the Molehole Mystery Club? This will entitle you to receive your very own Molehole Mystery Club ID card and Dusty's free newsletter. The newsletter will be filled with clues and mysteries you can solve and lots of fun things to do.

The newsletter will share things with you from God's Word that will help you live a happy life as a child of God. My spyglass shows me some wonderful words from the Bible that you need to remember always.

These verses are the Molehole Mystery Club Motto, and you will need to memorize them to become a member. The words are found in the Bible [1 Thessalonians 5:21 and 22]: "Test everything. Hold on to the good. Avoid [stay away from] every kind of evil" *(New International Version)*.

We'll be looking for your membership application for our club. See you in the next Molehole adventure story. Happy reading!

MOLEHOLE MYSTERY SERIES

Dusty and Musty are at it again, solving more mysteries. And you can be a part of the fun!

Join in with Dusty and the rest of the club and experience lots of neat adventures with them in **Dusty Mole, Private Eye; Secret at Mossy Root Mansion; The Gypsies' Secret; Foul Play at Moler Park; The Upstairs Connection;** and **The Hare-Brained Habit**.

All of the books in the Molehole Mystery Series are filled with the underground mystery and intrigue of your junior agent friends Dusty and

Musty Mole and the rest of the Mystery Club: Morty, Millard, Alby, Penney, Snarkey, Alfred, and Otis.

Don't let the villianous Sammy Shrew catch you by surprise. You can be on the inside track by joining the Molehole Mystery Club.

If you would like to be a member of the Molehole Mystery Club and hear more about the adventures of Dusty and Musty, fill out the card below and send it in. By being an official member, you will receive six issues of the newsletter, *The Underground Gazette,* and your own I.D. card.

- -

MOLEHOLE MYSTERY CLUB MEMBERSHIP APPLICATION

DATE:_____

NAME: _____

ADDRESS: _____

CITY, STATE: _____ ZIP:_____

AGE: _____ BIRTHDATE: _____

___ CHECK HERE IF YOU HAVE MEMORIZED
   OUR MOTTO VERSES,

1 THESSALONIANS 5:21 - 22.
"Test everything. Hold on to the good. Stay
away from every kind of evil."

Wait a minute, you mean the card is missing! Well you can still be a member of the Molehole Mystery Club by just sending in your name and address to:

Molehole Mystery Club
Lock Box 10064
Chicago, IL 60610-0064

Place
Stamp
Here

Molehole Mystery Club
Lock Box 10064
Chicago, IL 60610-0064